# CAN YOU FIND PUP? *

**I Like to Read**® books, created by award-winning
picture book artists as well as talented newcomers,
instill confidence and the joy of reading in new readers.

**We want to hear every new reader say, "I like to read!"**

**Visit our website for flash cards, activities, and more about the series:**
www.holidayhouse.com/ILiketoRead
#ILTR

**This book has been tested by an educational expert
and determined to be a guided reading level D.**

I LIKE TO READ is a registered trademark of Holiday House Publishing, Inc.

Copyright © 2018 by Vincent X. Kirsch
All Rights Reserved
HOLIDAY HOUSE is registered in the U.S. Patent and Trademark Office.
Printed and bound in April 2018 at Tien Wah Press, Johor Bahru, Johor, Malaysia.
The artwork was created with black gesso, graphite, and
watercolor on hot-press watercolor paper.
www.holidayhouse.com
First Edition
1 3 5 7 9 10 8 6 4 2

Library of Congress Cataloging-in-Publication Data
Names: Kirsch, Vincent X., author, illustrator.  Title: Can you find Pup? / Vincent X. Kirsch.
Description: First Edition. | New York : Holiday House, [2018] | Series: I like to read | Summary: Tate loves
to draw everything from cats to clowns but ignores his dog Pup, who runs away to join the circus.
Identifiers: LCCN 2017043231| ISBN 9780823439409 (hardcover) | ISBN 9780823439416 (pbk.)
Subjects: | CYAC: Drawing—Fiction. | Dogs—Fiction. | Lost and found possessions—Fiction. | Picture puzzles.
Classification: LCC PZ7.K6383 Can 2018 | DDC [E]—dc23 LC record available at https://lccn.loc.gov/2017043231

FOR MY DEAR FRIEND AND
TEACHER, JUNE MOON

# CAN YOU FIND PUP?

VINCENT X. KIRSCH

I Like to Read®

HOLIDAY HOUSE • NEW YORK

Tate likes to draw.
Pup likes to play.

But there
is no Pup.

Tate draws the garden.
Pup stands on his head.

# Can you find ten bugs?

tate

But there
is no Pup.

Tate draws the park.
Pup hangs from a tree.

# Can you find ten birds?

But there
is no Pup.

Tate draws the circus.
Pup juggles.

# Can you find ten clowns?

But there is no Pup.

Pup runs away.

Tate can't find Pup.

Tate is sad.
But here is Pup!

Tate draws and draws.

Can you find ten pictures of Pup?

And here
is Pup!

Pup finds Tate.
Now Tate will always draw Pup.